Pamela Camel

Bill Peet

Houghton Mifflin Company   Boston

At last a camel for my friends Bob and Blanche.

Library of Congress Cataloging in Publication Data

Peet, Bill.
  Pamela Camel.

  Summary: A tired and dejected circus camel finds long-
sought-after recognition along a railroad track.
  [1. Camels — Fiction. 2. Circus — Fiction. 3. Rail-
roads — Trains — Fiction] I. Title.
PZ7.P353Pam   1984   [E]   83-18594
ISBN 0-395-35975-9

Printed in the United States of America

RNF ISBN 0-395-35975-9   Reinforced Edition
PAP ISBN 0-395-41670-1

Y   10   9   8   7   6   5   4

Pamela Camel belonged to the Brinkerhoff Brothers Big Top Circus a long time ago. She was a scrawny scraggly camel who was much too clumsy and awkward to be a performer in the big top. And it saddened her to think that she could never be part of the big show, or ever do something clever or sensational to excite the crowds.

1

Otto the elephant trainer tried teaching Pamela to walk on a ball, but after teetering around for just a few seconds she lost her footing and came crashing to earth.

It was a painful lesson, and the poor camel was hurting from her scraggly hump on down to her toes for weeks afterward. So Pamela unhappily resigned herself to being an ordinary camel in the menagerie tent, to be stared at and insulted by the crowds on their way into the big top.

Everyone seemed to think that Pamela was exactly like all other camels, and to her dismay they called her a "bad-tempered beast," a "stupid brute," and "dumb as can be."

Pamela had to admit that she was indeed bad-tempered. But then, after all, anyone insulted as often as she was would be bad-tempered.

She was much more upset at being called stupid and dumb. But she couldn't prove the people wrong, since she couldn't perform tricks or do anything clever to show her intelligence. All she could do was remain aloof and suffer in silence.

Finally one day Pamela was fed up with all the insulting remarks and decided she had suffered enough. "I've had it up to here," she grumped, and with a furious jerk she snapped the flimsy rope that tied her to a tent pole.

It was in between shows in the late afternoon and everyone in the circus was catching up on his sleep, so slipping away was as easy as pie. As she tiptoed on out of the circus lot she was snickering to herself, "This is an awful waste of slyness, since no one in the show cares whether I'm here, there, or anywhere at all."

Once Pamela was free of the circus she headed off down the railroad track. It was a much safer way for a camel to travel than taking the highway with all the speeding autos, trucks, and buses. She knew it was sometimes hours before a train came chugging down the track.

Now that she was out on her own, Pamela had no idea where she was going. She just wanted to get away from it all, away from the circus crowds and all their unfriendly remarks.

She was loping along at a nice easy pace thinking how much fun it was to be way out in the country without a care in the world, when all at once she came across a break in the track.

"How dreadful," she said with a sigh. "What a shame. That break could cause a terrible train wreck."

The camel remembered passing the scene of a train wreck during her travels with the circus years ago. It was an awful disaster, with the engine upside down and the coaches all topsy-turvy.

Pamela was standing there on the track wondering what a camel could do to warn a train, when a great black cloud darkened the countryside and a zig-zaggedy streak of lightning shot across the sky, followed by a deep rumble of thunder. Storms terrified Pamela, and in an instant she forgot the broken rail and began searching wildly about for some kind of shelter.

Across an alfalfa field she spied a ramshackle old barn, and she made a dash for it, leaping through the wide-open door just as the storm cut loose in all its fury.

While Pamela was hiding in the barn waiting for the storm to let up, she got a bright idea. "I have no place to go," she thought, "so why don't I just stay here where it's peaceful and quiet and live off the tall grass growing in the field."

By nightfall the last rumble of thunder had faded away and the barn was indeed peaceful and quiet. There was only the skittering of the mice above on the rafters, and then the far-off *toot* of a train whistle.

Suddenly Pamela remembered the break in the track, and she was out of the barn like a shot!

As Pamela went galloping back across the alfalfa field, the train's headlight came flashing out of the night. It was coming full steam, CHUGGEDY-CHUGGEDY-HUFFETY-PUFFETY!! So there was no time to lose!

In frantic leaps and bounds Pamela was up the steep grade and onto the track, and when she reached the break in the rail she wheeled around to face the speeding locomotive.

16

"Now then," she muttered, "we'll soon see if the engineer will stop his train for a camel."

"What in blazes!" exclaimed the engineer when he caught sight of the camel ahead on the track. "What the devil is that dumb brute doin' out there?!!

Well, she'd better clear out — and quick, too! I'm not stoppin' this
train for one lousy camel! No siree!" And he gave her one last warning,
an ear-splitting blast with his whistle — TOOT! TOOT! WHOOT!
HOOT-AROO! WHOOIE!

But Pamela wasn't budging, and as the train kept coming full steam she shut her eyes tight to avoid the blinding glare of the headlight.

Then just when it seemed that the poor camel was done for, the engineer slammed on the brakes. There was a sudden grinding and screeching as the drive wheels skidded over the rails.

Then like some giant of a monster the huge engine shuddered and shook, it wheezed and rumbled and finally, with one mighty sigh, came to a halt, nose to nose with the terrified camel.

So the engineer *did* stop his train for a camel. But he was furious. He leaped from his cab and came storming past the engine with his fireman at his heels. "You dumb, dumb brute!" he shouted. "You stupid beast! You big dumb stupid brute!"

But all the insults in the world couldn't faze Pamela now. She had become so dizzy and weak from fright she fainted dead away and ended up sprawled on the track with her head resting on the broken rail.

"Hey! What's this?!" cried the fireman, pointing to the broken rail. "Just look at that piece of track!"

"Zounds!" exclaimed the engineer. "Maybe the poor brute was tryin'
to tell us something! Why, if we'd kept goin' full steam this old train
woulda gone cab over teakettle from here to kingdom come!! Zounds!!"

When Pamela finally recovered her senses and hauled herself back onto her feet, she was caught up in a wild celebration, as all the passengers swarmed off the coaches to express their gratitude to the heroic train-saving camel.

It was a tremendous triumph for Pamela, and in no time the news of her amazing display of courage spread throughout the land.

When the Brinkerhoff brothers discovered that the famous camel was theirs and had run away from their circus, they claimed her at once.

Pamela became a star attraction and led the grand procession into the big top at the start of every show.

And the ringmaster introduced her to the crowd as "THE ONE AND ONLY PAMELA CAMEL! THE MOST COURAGEOUS, THE MOST INTELLIGENT, THE MOST AMAZING AND EXTRAORDINARY DROMEDARY EVER TO WALK THE FACE OF THE EARTH!"

After the show, people came swarming around for a closer look at the fabulous camel, and for the very first time Pamela enjoyed the crowds and all the attention. After all, she had no need to worry about being called "dumb" or "stupid" ever again. And how could anyone call Pamela a "bad-tempered beast," now that she was all smiles and happy as a clam?